Rush

Of

Many

Waters

Also by Pauly Hart

Novels:
By the Gates of the Garden of Eden
Novellas:
Superior Respondent
Ouesso to Epena
The Book of Lesser Voices
Mountain to Mountain
The Word of Yahweh unto Enoch
Empire of the Dragon
Finance:
The Richest Man In Babylon Continued Stories
Collections:
Sometimes I Write Tiny Stories
Adelphoi
Poetry:
Stupid Mind Tricks
Book of Love and Laughter
The Cross and the Poet
What is Poep?
I Love You More Than a Fox Loves Blueberries
The Night Clerk Held a Broken Pencil
Spontaneous Psalms
Kick the Prick
Exegesis with Co-Authors:
My Flat Earth
Biblical Cosmology, 8+ languages
Translations:
The Testament of Job in Modern English
Children's:
Mathmagician and Other Tales of Awesomeness
Periodicals:
Modern Epistle (1-8)
Microzine (1-5)
Rush of Many Waters (1-20)
With children authors:
Farrell Family Fables
With Co-Author Jennifer Hart:
Adulting: A Daily Guide on Being an Adultier
Adult
Audiobooks:
Biblical Cosmology
Superior Respondent

Rush of Many Waters:

Volume One

By Pauly Hart

ISBN:978-1-955399-05-0
Library of Congress Catalog Data is available at: Loc.gov
This book is available at cost on Amazon.com and wherever fine books are sold.

Any references to historical events, real people, or real places are used fictitiously. Names, characters, and places are products of the author's imagination.
Front Cover Art by Franz Marc:
Front cover design by Pauly Hart

Paperback version printed in Savannah, Georgia, USA, where available.
First Edition, 2021
Author Contact: EmpiresAndGenerals@gmail.com
Author Website: PaulyHart.com

Contents

Shorts

A Problem of Coffins

Beginning Notes – A Greeting

To my dearest lord and savior, Parashaminalami,

All hail the overlord Kali in her good pleasure as she has seen fit to allow me to live yet another cycle of our moon. I owe my life to her good pleasure, to our great Archon, and the 365 spheres of her delight.

What follows are the notes of the dear late Natash, by his sometimes life partner and progeny born, Valparaiso of The Americas. Contained within are the last few entries in his last journal. I, his old friend Valparaiso, have collected these journal entries and tried to make the best sense of them for you, oh Parashaminalami. They were somewhat confusing, so I have broken them down into suitable chunks (or segments) so that none will be confused... Not that anything would ever be confusing to you, oh great one.

I was to meet our dear friend Natash today, this Elembivios (or Eilmí as it is sometimes called), at dawn, at Saint Andrews to celebrate with the Greater area Wiccan Coven. Thirteen thirteens of witches in all. There was to be a volunteer feeding, and possibly, if the right person presented herself, he was to turn his first centennial dhampir disciple this millennia. Alas it was not to be, and as such as the situation sits now, all engagements have been cancelled for both he and myself, as I have thrown myself headlong into the mystery surrounding his disappearance. Mayhap I can grasp at some answers in my searching.

I have only added this brief greeting at the beginning of my letter as a summation of what I have found, in this assemblage of the ramblings of this last remembrance of our late friend Natash, what you would call your humble servant. He knew of the old ways, and was always submissive, and had the old knowledge of our miraculous and stupendous history. His personal journal entries bear no date nor time to relate to anything that one would call a reasonable order. They are simply an account of his last days and how he spent them, and a few extraordinary events and accounts that transpired along his most recent time with us. There are some things that unfold that have no explanation. Yet, for the sake of continuity of the work, I have placed them in the most orderly manner possible.

This journal was gathered mostly from his manor, near Savannah, Georgia, where I now find myself. I had not seen him in over four seasons so I do not know how long he had been gone. It was a ramshackle manor, all but one of which was let out to renters, being split into a five-plex. There was the hallmark older colonial woodwork, mixed and mashed almost pell-mell into larger and more modern furnishings. No temptation into feng shui afflicted my friend in his renovations of this place. Large armoires here and there were combined with stainless steel trappings, and that was arranged inharmoniously with the decor of 1960's wallpaper and 1980's blonde wood floors. The renters were sheep, who knew nothing and could tell me nothing, but the house told me a little. As you know, I share one of the small gifts of the Apollonian, so I questioned the non-human inhabitants as to what may have happened to him. Most helpful was a Fiddleback who told me that it had been almost two whole moons since the dead one (meaning our Natash) had been seen.

And this is where I truly begin my tale. It is of one of us, a true Brahmaparusha, who lost his way, due to curious circumstances. But in the recounting, I would do ill if I thought that my interpretations would suffice, so, in order to do it the justice that it merits, it would behoove me to let our protagonist tell his own story and not edit the actual text, save for grammar and spelling. Though it grieves me to do such, to let his memoirs reach the eyes of someone other than his own self, I must do so – that his truth be known.

Segment – Coffin, Metal, and Christopher Lee

"Have a happy and merry, fun and jolly, merry, merry Tuesday." the facebook post read. Simple. So Slen did not celebrate Christ-mass. That was really all I needed to know. He didn't have to rub it in my face. Catholics can be such idiots. They don't even know when the Sabbath is. But I had other plans to think about. Tonight I was going to try my new experiment, and I hope it worked out as well as I think it should.

The immediate plan was not to take place at this moment, for it was the time of the sun, and I must retire to my casket to regain my life through the dark. My casket, made of Indonesian Teak, lay waiting. The long dark planks, fitted together by a memorial maker in Djakarta, had been my favorite this century. I had paid for it handsomely and here it was, calling me to retire into another day of escape.

The coffin was longer than usual, for I am an unusually tall person. I am 2.4 meters in height. Men balk when they see me for the first time usually, when I am first risen in the night. When I was young, I would wear the classic vestures of "Count Dracula" and I would get no ready customers. But I am wiser now and plunge men's minds into the fog and though they may look up at me at my unusual height, they seem not to notice the particulars of it. It seems to them that I am quite normal, and that there is nothing odd about me.

Because men are sheep. They are, for the most part, drinks to be sipped with the greatest of delights. Not all men are this way, mind you. Some men are reborn with The Christ, and they are the hardest to pierce. Ah, not that my teeth or my fingers have lost their edge, but it is the Spirit that dwells within them that gives them their power. I almost drink no men who have the Spirit, but when I do, I dine with delight.

I was speaking of my coffin though, and I digressed away from it like a man. I apologize.

Each tree has a life and story of its own and this Indonesian Teak is no different. The wood grows with the life that is given it from where it was planted. My teak was harvested on Irian Jaya, where the world is still wild with the lusts of the primitives. My tree was one of special delight, for it grew in blood of sacrifice. Where the fetishes of men waxed deep with their hatred of their neighboring tribe, they had slit the feet and genitals of their enemies and left them to bleed out into the roots of this marvelous old god of the forest.

The fresh Mayim and old Shemesh had given this tree a particular feel as well. Lizards and insects and who knows what else died and lent their spirits to the folds of the bark, and the tree had grown tall and fit. I had heard of the harvest of this great wonder and had hired the casket maker to acquire the materials from it for my coffin. The dark lusts bled through the wood and made it intoxicating in every way. It was a joy to touch.

The bottom panel was the heart of the tree, it was strangely lighter in color than all parts of the other planks, and there was a cracked seam that ran the entire length. The men who had planed the boards had specific instructions to leave the heart alone, for it was cracked. They were going to cut it and seam it together, but I found out about their plans and flew down to their workshop to stop them. I almost killed them, but I calmed myself and told them to leave it alone, for the flaw was part of the story of the wood. They plugged it with sawdust from the cut around the top, sealed it with the sap of the Guggul tree, and made it smooth.

The design was not sarcophagus style, with the loose lid that could be thrown back. It was a unique side-hinged device, with the hinge working off the bottom part of the side, from shoulder to toe-board. My coffin was not lined, or designed with copper or gold or silver. I had no dirty metals in use either. None of the designs of men over the smelting pot had any love from me. Though they mixed brasses and alloys and various steels with all their imaginations, none of these concoctions held any love from me. The hinges on the coffin were made of ironwood, fitted together using the old techniques.

My affinities were my own however. I only knew of one or two other purists among the fold. The brass family was a love of ours. Amusingly, many of the fold loved the faux silvers. Cupronickel swords and buttons and fasteners were all the rage during the 1960's. This was in part due to the sweeping fever with our kind from those in power in Hollywood. The man Christopher Lee had appeared in the 1958 movie: "Horror of Dracula" and after this, a wave of vampire movies swept the nation of the great United States of America.

I would tell you more of Christopher's involvement with our kind but he has just recently passed (anything less than 100 years is still recent to our kind). So I shall not slander him or his name with any stories. But from 1958 to 1976, that his face was your world's only relation to the people that is my kind, is not lost on us. Our love for him is that of deep, abiding respect. Man though he was, he promoted us in the spirit of our beloved Bram Stoker.

Segment – Margin Notes

It's not like Brahmaparusha need sleep or anything. We don't. It's the pineal gland that needs to recharge. Like most animals, we have ours intact but it works much differently now than when we were but base men. The pineal gland produces serotonin. This helps give men sleep and affects your entire nervous system. We Brahmaparusha are basically a sufferer from an endocannabinoid system mess, as well as other strange afflictions since our transmogrification into the greater gods that we are today.

The Pineal gland also handles photoreceptors, hence, we cannot abide in the sunlight. Most of our Endocrine system functions differently, as well. The Thalamus, Thymus, Thyroid, and Pituitary glands are what you would call: "wonky." So, when you hear stories of us ripping open the heads of our victims, it was mostly so we could get at the Pineal, Thalamus, and Pituitary. We don't actually eat the brains of our victims. That's disgusting. We just harvest certain parts. If we need Thyroid or Thymus, we simply rip out their neck. Science really.

Lest I forget - I have come across a man in the Masonic Order of the old Templars who has readily agreed to supply me with as much Adrenochrome as I wish. I am to meet him two days after the morrow.

Segment - Continued explanation of the coffin

In doing some quick research, I have inappropriately related to you my dealings in Indonesia. Evidently, they've changed names of places again. Djakarta has now lost its silent D and Irian Jaya has lost its ever so lovely and unique name and gone to the most boring name of West Papua. How droll their government systems must be… How insipid. But I would not stay there except to tell you of the purposes of my beautiful casket...

And I have failed in that regard, for few Vampires write. Wait. Is that the first time I've used that word? No, I used it before when I talked about Christopher Lee. That is fine, because that is what we are. I am the night king who dines on the lives of men who walk the earth.

This generation and the use of the word: "men." It was a month ago that I ran into this argument with my friend, another vampire, named Herbert. His name is odd, but in 1929 when he was made, it was quite a popular name, so I must forgive him that. I am off track again.

Writing! Bah!

At any rate, Herbert and I were having coffee and two youths got into an argument about the word. We placed their minds into a fog, lured them out into the night, raped them with rebar, and drank them like coconuts, but alas, we were hungrier afterwards than before we dined. The empty souls of man are not a meal. "Man" or "men" means "mankind." That the male of the species has this as the name as well is the way it just came to be. In the English tongue, fe-male or wo-man is not diminutive, but derivative. This seems to infuriate some, rather than educate and illuminate. There are a thousand things that people think of us that are completely false, and I wish I had the power to change their views on these images... But again, I have only come to realize that people are sheep to be drunk.

So... Where was I? Ah yes, my coffin. It is a lovely device, devoid of any trappings of comfort, for that would delegitimize its purpose. It was plain and bare and smelled of the old world. Some vampires, having not undergone the full transformation into their true selves are stuck within the coffins drifting off into a listless slumber where they are somehow able to achieve human sleep. These half -blood Satanists drift away into their dream world and let the opportunities of the day escape them fully. For the fully actualized Master, like myself and so many of the other masters, spend this time in a loose spirit travel, something akin to the yogi masters of Hinduism. We are of the same family - Hindus and Vampires... At least we serve the same gods.

Segment - Margin Notes

There is one aspect of the Brahmaparusha that is not known to most, and that is the need for the Adrenal gland, specifically the Adrenochrome that can be harvested from it, as well as from the brain stem. Most of us just like to eat the adrenal glands raw, but there are some of us more endowed with the understanding of chemistry. Several communes in Romania offer all of these substances in over the counter doses, but those of us in the real world have to go about it in the old way. I understand now that even our Illuminati brothers are using Adrenochrome in their rituals. Ah. Refreshing to watch the puppets in their escapades.

Gone are the old ways of the Asura possessions, the coming in, the cocaine use, the dying and resurrecting... That may be how the foolish Satanists still do it, but their only hope is to achieve that of the nosferatu - the disfigured ones... The cheaters. Real and still existing vampires come out of the past, and are immortal, and we only take on a few new souls at a time to transform. It's really out of boredom more than anything. We... I do not wish to rule. What fun is that? I hunt as a fox in the hen-house, as it were. I do not wish to rule the chickens.

We Nephilim are a sordid bunch really. And people laugh that we call ourselves Nephilim. But where do they think we came from? Have they not read any of the Bible? Enoch? The Book of Giants? The epic of Gilgamesh? The daughters of men lay with the sons of god, and thus were born the adversaries. And of that tree, we are but one small branch.

Here I speak of astral projection in its purest sense. There are only a few who will take to the skies to travel and meet in accords and gatherings around the world. Few of us there are, for few of us really hold to the old ways that made us who we are today.

We must, as a vampire society, come back to the roots of our pure religion. For it was that we intend and we strive and plead with the old ways and the old masters, to do something that we are not supposed to do. If we would just realize our true callings and act beholden to them, we could have enslaved man by now.

But it is not to be. Many of my kind will disagree with me but The Christ will win in the end. Though they deny it, we all know this deep down, but it is our chief desire to rail against Him of Heaven. And now I must write this reverie to myself... To tell a story of great delight and some dismay. Delight in that, I see our true purpose, dismay in that, I also see that no one wants to adhere to it any longer. Woe to us, night born, for we diminish in the light of the new and coming antichrists.

It was December and Shemesh was a half hand from rising... I was "off to bed" as they say. Saying farewell to my venus fly traps, I lay down in the coffin I had before this one (an old cedar monstrosity from Lebanon) when I dove deep into my mind and pulled back the realm of flesh to spring out of my body into the world in my spirit form. This usually takes only a few minutes, as I am a practiced projector, but for some reason it took me longer than normal.

I did not understand what was taking so long until the very last second when I was making the turn into spirit - what some call "fog." I had not known what it was until the very last moment, for when I rose up out of the casket in spirit, I was greeted by one of His messengers. This was frightening enough, and, adding to the fact that he had his sword drawn, I was terrified. If I were mortal, I would have either shat my pants or fainted dead away.

I did reel and scream like a mewling fool of a little girl, but quickly recovered and lowered my hands. Though he could have slain me in the coffin, he had not taken action against me. He stood as a statue, not moving, his bright golden eyes remaining fixed on my every movement. His ivory sword was still in his hand, with the flame residue dripping like wax into the air before sizzling away into nothingness. *Veoyyy veoyyy.* The drips gave foleys to his stillness.

"What wanteth thou oh messenger?" This came out of my mouth readily, for most angels speak in the King James English, as did we when we encountered them.

He said nothing immediately, but slowly he sheathed his sword and drew out a living scroll from his side. A living scroll was not a joke. It had come from the commands of Heaven itself, and could not be refused. Not by me nor by anyone. If you were given a living scroll, it was to be followed whether you were in submission or agreement.

It floated to me as if in water and landed in my hands.

Now, remember that I was still in my coffin below the spirit me. The silver thread that connected us was very visible now. If the angel had wanted to, he could have severed the line and killed me then and there, my days of life immortal would be over instantly. However, he had sheathed his sword and addressed my spirit directly. The scroll opened before me.

The words were of the pure tongue and he knew that I could not read it. Was this mockery or a warning? I did glance at it and knew that it was legitimate. Maybe this was his reason for waiting to speak, that I would know it was not a fakery.

It floated back to him, and he placed it once again on his side.

"Elizabeth Macleary." He said. "You are not to touch her, for behold, she standeth anointed." As he said her name, a face filled my mind. I saw a Laotian-American woman, twenty three, standing in a supermarket, directly after sunset. She turned, saw me, and screamed. Then the vision went away.

His face came back to view. Stern and humorless. He was a stocky sort. The kind you find no humor with, nor do they find any humor with anything. I had met his kind before. All work and no play. How boring. And now that I knew he could not harm me without provocation, I would toy with him a little.

"Who is thine commander?" I asked him. I knew he did not owe me an answer, but he told me nonetheless.

"I am of Sakoz, of Jarnosh, of Kebar, of Uriel." He said, and puffed out his chest. There, on his left chest, where a human heart would beat below, stood his rank and insignia. Strange. I had not seen this one before. It was a golden foot crushing an alligator's head.

"An alligator? Is that not a little dull?" I asked, smiling.

"Behold!" he said. And with that word, I suddenly understood. It was not a lowly swamp dweller after all. It was Leviathan.

I recoiled immediately upon the revelation, but anger flared up within me almost as quick.

"Knowest who thou mocks?" I flared up, floating up to the ceiling, showing my full height.

"Knowest who thou challenges?" His sword was in his hand again, his wings flapped open quicker than a blink. His face matched my face and we stood apart almost nose to nose. My legs were almost two feet below his, for again, he was a stocky sort. His short black hair was cut close, modeled after the fashion of Hellenistic Greece and, even in my spirit form, I could smell incense from the Altar. This was an elder, to be sure. He must be old, to be this tough.

I backed down slowly, raising my hands up at my side, and came close to the floor again. Although I did not need to, I bowed. I didn't want to fight this angel; he would have killed me in seconds. I knew when I was matched, and indeed, overpowered. The spirit body, even the mortal body I possessed would never be able to match his, and I was wise to know it.

"Let it be as thou sayest." I said, eyes to the floor. I felt the heat of his sword flare up then disappear, and before long I looked up and he was gone, absorbed into the air around me.

Segment – Margin Notes

With Vampires, there is blood. There is always blood. Usually most of the requirements we need are in the blood. But sometimes for us there is a feasting of the glands... And if it comes from either human or an unclean animal, the former is always preferred. When a human is not available, swine blood is a good substitute. Oh. And there are many varieties of both on the menu, but humans do have one distinction that I will offer now before I move on to the main thrust of this letter. Virgins taste better. And the younger the virgin, the tastier. I recall attending a meeting with the Bohemian Grove and there was a pure, three year old girl there, an actual virgin, I must say. Not even a hint of sodomy from the red shoe clansmen. I admit that a frenzy overcame me and I ate most of her, flesh and all. It was most tasty. Even the meat had a taste that I have not had since the 1400's at Stonehenge. I was not invited back. But I digress.

Our bodies don't have the proper serotonin or melatonin. So we avoid the sunlight primarily for this reason, that we cannot handle it. Sunlight actually makes us violently ill. It's not as you picture it in Hollywood movies at all. They've got it all wrong. Most have it all wrong about vampires, specifically, the Brahmaparusha. It all comes down to the Torah and the evil found therein. There it is. I've gone and spilled the beans about the reality that lies at the heart of it all. It's one of the reasons that I enjoy swine blood. Swineflesh, to me, is the most non-Kashrut I could think of… Except maybe the aborted.

To not be confusing to myself on re-reading, I will clarify. Torah is the law of God for Israel. Kashrut is the diet law found inside the Torah. So simple. Certain mystics try to change the diet laws into something called: "Kosher" but it's all a lie. Just ask a cheeseburger if it's a goat and a kid – That's homework for most.

Segment – Separate page, insert

I recall being told that we were first introduced to Europe by the Diadochi kingdom of Seleucus, where we began to travel westward. Some of us went north to what would become China, but this is not the story of the Jiang Shi, and the soul sort. They moved into another realm and devolved… Or evolved… It depends on who you ask.

Not me. Degenerates one and all.

Migration was easy enough, if you knew who to hire. So we made it to the Capitol of the Seleucid Empire, what was then called Antioch, and eventually moved north to what is now Romania. We have spread out from there. Chicago, New Orleans, Paris, Moscow, and Tokyo. Now here I am, in Savannah Georgia, writing this. So let me get on with it.

The coffin is the best piece of furniture for blocking out the sun. Oh it gets very boring, mind you… "Sleeping" in a coffin. Mostly I meditate and place myself under a spell. At times, if the mood fits me, I go into a trance and astral project my spirit to other places. This is more fun, but is very taxing and I can only do it if I "went to bed" on an empty stomach. You see, with our malady, the hungrier you are, the more power you have. The fuller you are, you are still absorbing the matter from your host into yourself, and the less of "you" there is to be you.

I have more to write. I need to buy a journal - I shall do this on the morrow.

Segment Four - Information

I have been bothered recently by the curious, unfolding day of the scroll. I let the day take me and slept through the night, and awoke inside the coffin the next day and the next. Getting my spirit ready, I leapt out into the third day, my mind very anxious to have answers. I travelled above the clouds and heading west and north toward Chicago, where I felt I would find my cabal ready and anxious about my being missing. Things were never less true. Only Indigo Dark Burn, wandering spirit,was there to meet me. Of the others in our order I knew not. Indigo was a second spirit in the middle rite, a fully fallen devil of the stars. I did not like him and he knew this, yet here he was, the only one present. I acknowledged him.

"What are you about today?" I asked.

"Here and there I wander. Here and there I learn." he said in his obnoxious poetic ramble.

I hated this foul spirit.

"Where are the others?" I asked him. "Selth? Is he not with you?" I asked of his counterpart, for the two were always together these days.

"Gone he is. Back to fire, banished down. Down, ever down he floats into dark." The devil looked sad. This was news indeed. Selth did not serve the Darker Lords in obedience, he was like Indigo, a wandering devil, but fully fallen - reticent, yet submissive.

"Who cast him down?" I asked.

"The Legion who tramples Leviathan. They come and cast. I escaped because of sympathy, or pity, or fear of my many pleadings." he said, truthfully.

He was never this truthful. Something changed him.

"Were you shown a scroll?" I asked, looking at him squarely.

He acted like he had been hit and recoiled away from me, screaming a long whine.

I rushed to him and grabbed him by the throat. His small neck fit easily into my hand. I could crush it if I wanted, but it would not hurt him I knew.

"Tell me of the scroll!" I commanded.

"You are not my lord!" he whined. "I need not tell you of these things, for I float long and…"

"Quiet!" I commanded. He shut up.

I let him go. His leathery wings groomed his neck where my hands had been. Silver wisps of smoke trailed and fell away from his neck as he brushed himself from his faux bruisings.

"Go, I must." he said softly and angrily, like a scolded child. He spun twice like a top and shot out over the clouds, leaving no wake behind in the natural world.

He was powerless. He did not even make wind to affect the water in the air. What a hated fool. I had wasted my time in coming.

I looked down below me, for I dare not look up. From this far up, you could make out the feet of those unfallen. They were always above. So was He, and I did not wish to look at Him.

Spread out before me, a disc with upturned edges, the earth shown blue and green. I needed to get back. It was already growing late. Time worked differently here. Sometimes hours were minutes but today the minutes seemed to have been hours. There were ways to control this, but I had not learned them yet.

Segment - A night for giving and dining

I awoke two hours before sunset, fully refreshed from feeding yesterday on a nice prostitute and her john. I stripped down to nakedness and gave myself a loofa bath and a Halo hair treatment, and put on my best Givenchy Bathrobe. It was December the 21st and I meant to make the most of it. Tammuz would want her death to be a happy celebration. And what closer time to idolatrize the Catholic god than good old Christmas. I had purchased a Santa Claus outfit last month and had it sent to my tailor, Claude, directly after getting some measurements. It put it on, and it fit like a glove. Rather than have the ordinary paunch that Old Saint Nick has, I opted for the skinny terrifying version. As I have mentioned before, I am lean and I made quite the spectacle in any outfit.

I decided to take it to the next level. Might as well be dapper. Tonight would be the continuation of a glorious Saturnalia for me. Almost as good as All Hallows Eve… The only night of the year I really let loose. "Christ-Mass" has become a second glorious night for me. And this year was going to be full of adventure.

Every vampire has skill sets. The uniqueness of our skills is as varied as our bodies are. Some vampires that I know have bulging bodies in excess of several thousand pounds. Much larger than any human would have ever believed. Some of us fly, some of us bend human wills, and some of us have lycanthropy. I have a very small skill set. My main skill is to bend human senses. It is indeed a very narrow skill yet I use it with great acumen. And not many have my skill. I have learned how to make a mass effect towards groups of people, making them all believe that they were going through an earthquake. When they look, most see me as an old woman. I have not yet learned how to be invisible, but I have managed to get by with becoming a Pomeranian. That was oh so very tiring.

Many of my brothers and sisters can fly in their mortal bodies, some have long fingernails or teeth that can retract and grow at will. Some who cannot fly, can run or move at great speed. While we can all move faster than the normal human, I am one of the slower ones. Some say my skills are low, and yet, can they clear out a building because everyone smells smoke?

So it was with my skills that I grew even taller in man's eyes and made my face exaggerated with the gauntness that is my norm. Pale eyes, white hair, an almost translucent green pallor - I was quite the sight, and I was ready to hit the town. Watch out Forsyth Park, Santa Zombie is coming.

Once I was ready, there was nothing holding me back from going for a nice walk down the street. I live in downtown Savannah, an area that most consider historic. I will not tell you where really, for I do not know who will ever come to find me.

Consider that, you vampire hunters. Come and find me if you dare, for I will rip you in half. But, if you know anything at all about Savannah, you will know that most of the downtown area is "historic" - Most of the squares are "historic" - most of the graveyards are "historic" and all of the hated humans deem them to be "haunted." Oh, if only they knew.

Segment – Margin Notes

I grow weary of talking of my own kind, and yet I find that I must, for the popularity of the subject comes and goes like the fleeting psithurism. Here a whoosh, next a whisper, next there is nothing. And that is our tale with them. We are naught but fleeting imaginations for them to ridicule. If they saw us for what we were, they would die in their sins on the spot. Every movie they've ever seen only shows the weakest of us, in our most obnoxious form. They know nothing. Tonight I will take her.

Segment – Last Entry

The battle may have been my last. Elizabeth Macleary was more protected than I believed her to be. I do not believe that I have much time. Valparaiso, if you find this book, know that this edition is but the latest…

THEY ARE HERE!

End Notes

And so there ends the only tale that I have from his pen. This is the only edition that I have found in all of the articles that Natash kept in his small room. The last segment, which is brief and unfinished and ending ominously with "THEY ARE HERE" is of great import to my very soul, for if it was the Messenger Sakoz, then one might say that there is a bit of a problem… For, as you know, great lord, the angelic blade is one of the only real ways to dispatch one of our kind, but in order to do so, you need special permissions…

As I understand it, and correct me if I am mistaken, you need a very specific form (or scroll as their kind calls them), and it has to be filled out very precisely. But that is indeed the wrench in the works. If Natash is a free spirit and a soul with a will of his own, then how did the permission get written? Inside each form is an exact time and place, and situation that must occur, in order for the dispatch to take place. Literally the year, season, moon cycle, and where the sun is all need to be mentioned specifically, or the form is invalid. That's precision, and that's horrifying. This startling accuracy in his execution, nay, assassination, is unequivocal to me.

And it leads me down a philosophical journey, so to speak. I have to begin with the premise that Natash was assigned to be dispatched. So then all of the things that led him to the exact moment of his demise would have had to have been seen aforehand by some all-knowing force.

There is only one explanation: He himself must have seen to it that Natash be eliminated. There is no other logical way to provide answers for this scheme. Unless the Book of Knowledge had it listed as an "inevitable", then I cannot fathom any other way for the scroll (form) to have been activated.

This is gravely terrifying. It sets me to wonder about my own future. Are we all to be vanquished just as easily?

I pray this letter and the accompanying sets of notes have met your grace with the approval that I deemed it would seek, and I pray that the knowledge, nay, wisdom found herein would be a boon to you on this, the blessed day of our Satan.

With warm regards, Valparaiso of the Americas

Poems

Charcoal Man

It was on a middle floor maybe.
One long hallway and a bedroom near the end that I was on.
At the other end was a doorway with a door that came up from the floor that led a stairway down.
She was in stairway.
Black hair and gray dress.
And he was in the bedroom, at my end of the hall.
Tied to the bed.
Not tied so much maybe.
His left arm had a large metal hinged spike through it.
She would turn the hinge and he would scream.
Gruesome and bothersome.
His eyes, red with burst blood, angry.
But he cut off the arm above the elbow, nearer to the bicep so the door would crush her.
I didn't realize that she was the evil one until too late.
But earlier he had me cut off his pinky on his right hand so she could fight the evils on the lower floor.
And I had begged him not to make me.
But the more you inflicted pain upon the man...
The more power he had to defeat the evils on the lower floor.
He had already sawed off his own legs.
And when she would leave him she would do so in the name of love and go down the hallway to fight.
Fight the dread.
And the door would go into the floor.
And she would turn with a blank and hesitant look, over her left shoulder.
And tell him that she loved all of him.
But I had to be there now.
For he had no one left to cut him.
So he drew me and made me.

The Charcoal Man.

He had summoned me from the floor to cut him.

She would return.

Blood up to her elbows.

And she would walk the hall.

Hair distraught.

Arms painted red.

Dripping in the hallway.

And she would wash there, in the sink in the room of the man on the bed.

A large metal sink without a counter.

The kind that butchers have.

A large oaken butcher block.

She says that she knows that he is anxious.

His black hair and dark eyes.

And his mouth sewed shut.

His eyes cry. They do the pleading.

She knows that I am there but says nothing.

She knows that he has summoned me.

Summoned me to cut off his left arm.

For he cannot.

Be strong , she tells him, the battle is almost won.

And then it is loose with a jerk.

And there is a new stain upon the ceiling.

And she folds the skin over and stops the flow.

And takes the arm and places it into the floor where the teeth are.

And breathes deeply.

She goes back down the hallway to the door on the end she came from.

It slides down and lets her in.

You must take my eyes while she is gone, he tells me.

I cannot do this thing.

His eyes are all he has left.

He lost his ears long ago.

But she needed me to see everything, he tells me.

Now that my arm is gone, I understand, he tells me.

Now that you are here, I understand, he tells me.

Take my eyes quickly, and I dig in, black ash hands crumbling.

Nothing.

Take the scoop, he says.

There on the side of the metal bed, a scoop.

And I dig into the charred socket.

Place it in the floor where the woman placed me, he says.

The teeth, yellow and hungry, take the eye.

The woman screams down the hall.

What are you doing? She calls down the hall.

But the door is sliding up, catching her.

She cannot move now, she is pinned to the ceiling.

The dirty yellow wallpaper shakes as she screams.

Quick the other one, he tells me.

I am hesitant.

It is the only thing left of him.

Do it, he pleads.

Do it not, she screams.

The other eye comes out easier than the first.

It goes into the mouth...

Almost.

With it still in hand, I look out the doorway of the man's room, down the hallway.

Her face is downcast, but it is dripping blood.

The same eye that I took from the man is now missing in her head.

She sees me and laughs.

I did not feed the man's other eye into the mouth.

She lifts her hand and the eye from my hand is in the air.

It moves on its own.

I reach out and grab it.

Her hand is there with her.

Stuck on the ceiling, she calls to it and it tries to leave me.

I know you can hear me bitch! The man cries.

You shall never have all of me! He cries.

She laughs.

The eye has broken through my hand and now floats to her with my ash fingers still clutching it.

She brushes my fingers away and places it in her head where the other eye had been removed.

And pushes the door back down, full of new-found strength.

She floats so slowly down the hall.

Now all that remains is to feed my children, she says.

And the door at my end of the hallway opens.
Not the room I am in, the door at the end.
It too, slides from the top downward.
And as her children feed on the man, he might have been saved.
He had no legs or arms or tongue.
And I am all that is left of him.

Jesus Northstar

Guide me ever-onward Father
    Touch me with your wondrous might
Pull me like you pull your compass
    Treat me like you treat your children

Jesus Northstar, guide me onward

Electric Life, I'm charged with your love
    Give me signs that I'm on course
Hold me, touch me with wholeness
    Bring me closer to your fire

Store me in your life-sized wonder
    Break me on your rocky shore
Hold me till the noon-tide washes
    shield me in every way

Tighten jigs and pull them tautly
    Batten hatches in my soul
Trim the sails and hold them steady
    Pull me into life's' hard tide

Jesus Northstar, pull me ever

Jesus Northstar, your my light.

Various times

More often than not,
Have I ever once thought,
I would be in a place such as this.

And at various times,
With the wind through the chimes,
I could love you so much more than this.

Though you knew me the same,
Knew my faults and my gains,
Even the split hairs on my head.

I sure love you my Lord,
As the strings on a chord,
play your sweet tune in my head.

Your smile

There were some things
I wanted to share
I don't know where
to go from here
Today is taking too long
Life goes on and on
I've got to find a reason
For this same old song

There is no time like the present
To wash all of my troubles away

There is no place other than in your arms
To take away the fear, to take all of my pain

It's your smile baby... That gets me through the day.

?

Thoughts of a related time and place have enveloped my journey here. I have fallen prey to the undisciplined practice of living in the "what if" syndrome. I see my days march along and wonder what consequences would befall me if i had done this or done that. i realize that this way of thinking is a corrupt way, and to be more precise... it is an unhealthy view on the universe in general. Shouldn't i be more concerned with the here and the now... but there i go again. i keep doing this to myself. the now is what i live in. not the past, or any alternate reality in this present, or even in the impending future. i plan and schedule, but it is the now that i function within. so i make plans to not make plans. striving for a future where my present consists of whole-hearted plans of the now. the now. the here.

The beginning of my life.

```
things bug me
```

things bug me...
like
cigarette smoke
on a cold day
like
naked women
in my pure mind
like
hypocrites lying
instead of forgiving
like
people flaming
not understanding

like
when i get cut off
in a turn lane
like
when i ramble
like
now.

Essays

A Brief Study

John, the Rabid Oscillating Weasel, was finishing up his free bowl of chili - smacking all the while. JB had been lounging in the booth, but reluctantly gave up his seat as I sidled up. The waitress sat down and proceeded to explain.

"Take out a sheet of paper and a pin," she said

"Don't you mean PEN?" I asked.

"Yeah whatever," she said.

"I'm just saying that you pronounced it incorrectly."

"Do you want to do this or not?" her face scowling.

"Sorry." I said.

Pens and pins ready, she explained.

"All you need to do is define what words I will tell you."

"Like an explanation?" I asked.

"Like a *definition*," She repeated.

"*Geaaaaw*!" JB retorted, "Don't you ever pay attention?"

"Ok guys, she said... ready?"

"Yeah." We said.

"Okay, the first item is a cube."

"You mean... like..."

"Tell me what it looks like. One sentence, no more than a paragraph."

The Cube: It's clear, one of its sides is actually a tiger and it's being held by Martin Luther, and King Jr.'s face is on the opposite side. Inside the cube is a pink cloud with a lonely purple teardrop that drips down onto this very paper. Upon the very farthest corner of the cube sits a very small herd of yaks.

"Done," I said.

"FINALLY!" they all said.

I looked around and discovered that they had been done quite some time ago.

"Ummm, I think mine is too long."

Looking bemused she looked down at my paper. Then at the others. JB had something like: "Big and red." Or John's single sentence, alluding to his cube being sleek and shimmering.

"The next object is a ladder," she said.

"Describe it on your paper."

I looked down. Hmmm. Not as interesting as a cube, I said in my own head, but oh well.

The Ladder: The ladder is made of rough cardboard, and of very small ground up bacon bits. It is covered in celtic spirals and leading towards an orange bush. Of course it is flat on the ground.

Hmmm. That wasn't tough. I actually got done before JB was finished thinking and doing what appeared to be some oral surgery with the back of his pen. Something like realization dawned upon his rugged and good looking face. He finished up his answer.

"Next is the horse," she said.

"A horse?" John asks.

"Yes, a horse. Then a storm." She says.

The Horse: The most beautiful horse in the world was vandalized by ghetto graffiti artists. It was the most majestic and comely purple, but now is a horrid slur of dingy browns. She looks terrible. She has been hurt very badly in the past and has a limp in her left front leg and has gone blind in her left eye. But a horse like this cannot be stopped, for she thinks that she is the strongest horse in the entire universe.

The Storm: The storm was coming from one of feather clouds that was inside the cube. It rained down over large blue and yellow marshmallows. They fell about the same speed you would expect marshmallows to fall in your dreams. It was very odd. They were immediately devoured by odd little leprechauns before they ever hit the ground.

John had been watching me write the last one, and said that it would be a great movie to see. I asked what he meant.
"The new movie Being Pauly Hart."

I looked at him and crossed my eyes. "MALCOVICH MALCOVICH," in my most loony voice.

He smiled.

"Are we done?" JB asks.

"Nope." She was laughing. "Two more. OK?"

OK's echoed all around.

The Flowers: At one time there were exactly 1,543,297,208 flowers. They encompassed the entire range of mountains and fields of plains within my mini-vision. But the horse had eaten all but three of them. The three left are small thick dark yellow tulip-type flowers, and they smell of rotting strawberries. The three that are alive have developed electro-anti-horse-neutrino rays in self-defense so that they can survive.

"What was next?" John asks.

"The relationship," she says.

"Of matter versus antimatter?" I asked.

"Of Heather Locklear to Former President Clinton?" said John.

"No," she said, "But I'd like to see that last one." Chuckles from John and myself. JB said that it wasn't funny.

"As former Commander In Chief, Clinton should have..." Yada yada...

"Yeah, shut up." I said.

"What in the world are you talking about anyway?" John said.

"What do YOU MEAN?" JB said.

"Guys!" She had to break in and thank God she did. "The relationship of all of these things to one another." A pause.

"*Oooooooh*," we all said at once.

The Relationship: As stated before without prior knowledge of the relationship factor, the storm exists inside the cube. Upon this knowledge, the cube exists inside the horse's mind, but as explained before, the horse is on the same plane as the flowers. And these of course, are on the ladder... or within the second rung of the ladder to be exact. This would mean that the horse and the flowers would have to be very very tiny.

"Done." I said.

"Really?" She said.

"Yup." I said.

"Ok." She said.

"What was the point here?" John said.

"Oh, just have some FRIKKIN PATIENCE CADET!" JB booms.

"Oh can it jar-head..." She said.

Lots of laughing.

"Alright gentlemen," she pronounced. "Here is what each item stands for:"

"The cube is yourself.
The ladder is your friends.

The horse is your lover.
The storm is your problems.
The flowers are your children."
And their relationship? I wondered.
"It's to one another." She says, reading my mind.
She gave us our ticket, and walked away, her hair, an auburn sunset.

Swimming Pool Baptism

So there I was, sopping wet and sanctified, having undergone the commandment by Jesus to show a sign of repentance and salvation by being submerged underwater. Pretty funny, but also very effective. I couldn't have come up with something so clever if I had tried. Anyway. There's a powerful truth behind it and it seems to work out well in the spirit world. I don't really know how, but then again, I'm just a guy and He's God. I don't really have to understand how things work, I just need to submit. Anyway, it was at that point that I really believe things started to change in my heart. I really did have a life changing experience mentally and spiritually. My mind was "awoken" and my heart was "quickened" within me. It was awesome. I also spoke in other tongues, but that's a story for another book.

My family was attending a small Charismatic church in Wichita, Kansas and we were happy with it. My little brother and I were in "Children's Church," which was pretty close to a lively version of Sunday School. We had fun. There were lots of puppets and it was like a party. Pastor Paul and Mike and Peggy were really good at helping us kids understand about who God was and how He was real and how our lives could be changed with His spirit. They filled our minds full of Bible stories and charged our hearts full of faith. And at the same time, I had started studying the Bible for myself. I remember it like it was yesterday. I started reading my mom's Living Bible Edition. It was large and had a green leather cover and smelled like cheese.

One day I happened upon a story from the book of Joshua. Obviously I didn't get there on my own. I had heard the story in Children's Church and decided to check it out for myself. There it was. In black and white. "Sun, stand still at Gibeon, and moon, in the Valley of Aijalon." (ESV) Joshua had asked God for a miracle and He had performed it. Of course it was real and of course it happened. I was ten years old and I believed God at His word so of course it happened.

My father, a scientist of the geologic persuasion, told me that it was a metaphor. The earth had stopped rotating. Maybe it had only seemed to be stopped. Maybe it was an eclipse and Joshua was mistaken. Maybe Joshua was wrong. Maybe something else happened. But then how did anyone explain the next verse? "Is this not written in the Book of Jasher? The sun stopped in the midst of heaven and did not hurry to set for about a whole day." (ESV) Well. I wasn't "allowed" to read the book of Jasher back then but we did go round and round on the topic for a while. I finally ended up dropping the discussion. We never came to an agreement and I never brought it up again. I did, however, ask him about Hezekiah and when the sun went backwards.

"And Hezekiah said to Isaiah, "What shall be the sign that the YHVH will heal me, and that I shall go up to the house of the YHVH on the third day?" And Isaiah said, "This shall be the sign to you from the YHVH, that the YHVH will do the thing that he has promised: shall the shadow go forward ten steps, or go back ten steps?" And Hezekiah answered, "It is an easy thing for the shadow to lengthen ten steps. Rather let the shadow go back ten steps." And Isaiah the prophet called to the YHVH, and he brought the shadow back ten steps, by which it had gone down on the steps of Ahaz." 2 Kings 20:8-11.

Now, my mother had been the child of the very well-known missionary Hoyt Eudaly, who worked with the Southern Baptists in Mexico in Bible publishing. He had been wise and strict and had raised my mother with a very pragmatic and dogmatic viewpoint of the Word of God. Not a lot of room for miracles. Not a lot of room to question. I would never ask her anything theoretical, I didn't want to be seen as "being silly" in her eyes. But I never got an answer about Hezekiah from my dad or my Children's Church Pastors or anyone else. Some questions (it seemed to me as a child) were best left to dumb faith. Well I thought that was silly then and I think it's silly now. There is a scientific explanation to every miracle in the Bible. There always has been, and there always will be. We just need to understand the rules of the science that He uses to begin with.

A Fool and his Bible

"So, how are you with 'health and wealth.'?" Doris Howard asked me, at the back of the church sanctuary. The second service had ended, and we were catching up on old times.

"Oh, I suppose I want to be both." I said, ignorantly honest of her meaning.

She smiled and sighed. "Still the same old Paul that I knew. No, I mean, how are you with the prosperity message?"

My eyes widened. That was indeed a great question. How was I with that whole bag of tricks?

I thought for a brief moment of all that would be given me (or not given me) should I answer without really understanding what I would be (or not be) answering. The weight of the conundrum would be disenchanting to most young people, had they not already known Doris for the years that I did.

I spoke plainly and without tact, as was my custom then: "I mean, Jesus healed us by His stripes and He owns the cattle on a thousand hills. I suppose if He loves me, he'll give me my daily bread." I told her.

She leaned back and smiled. "That's a good answer."

I passed her test. I would speak to the young adults class the following Wednesday and would be in her good graces.

Doris Howard, champion of the faith, Youth Pastor extraordinaire, passed away not some time ago - but her words still echo in my mind. "That's a good answer." That quick statement still guides me on a daily basis. I want to give a good answer when I am questioned on my faith. I want to always give a good and Godly answer.

She asked me about the "message" concerning "health and wealth" and I gave her three scripture truths to defend my position. No clearer message about the message than the one already given me through the best text that I had reference to – yon B.I.B.L.E. Basic Instructions Before Leaving Earth.

Answering her question, I could have repeated some adages or some doctrinal statements from the Charismatic Seminary I was attending at the time in Tulsa, Oklahoma... But would that have really sat right with the great hyper-conservative Non-Denominational church, in Wichita, Kansas? "We're the most boringly normal Church you'll ever visit," is their motto. It would be years later, and I would find myself in a denomination loosely affiliated with them, and they were right. It was as vanilla as could be. I was a Youth Pastor in that denomination, and they had the basics of church down. Not too much of this, and not too much of that... So the real question became: Did the Wichita church love their Charismatic neighbors two and a half hours south of them? Did they love the message that was being preached so vigorously from the pulpits there? No. They did not love the "Health and Wealth Message."

But I didn't know that. Or at least I didn't see what the big deal was. I didn't get why we couldn't get along with one another despite the differences of our theological makeup. Oh my goodness, what a ignoramus I was. We should be able to get along with each other despite the slight variations of the interpretations of the Bible right? Not in the world that we live in. But I'm a dreamer, I suppose. I always expect the best. I have learned over time to not only expect the best, but I've learned to plan for the worst. My age has tempered my unabashed optimism with a dash of potentiality in realism.

Suddenly it was Wednesday night and there I was in front of a sea of young people that I had gone to "Youth Group" with. I had been the only Senior in High School at the group surrounded by the teeming throngs of youthful and hyper-adolescent faces who all looked up to me. It was a rather strange mix of kids my brother's age, all Freshmen and Sophomores. It had been just me as a Junior, the year before, with a gang of really cool Seniors one year above me. My friend at the time, Fletcher Booth, sharing the same birthday with me, instantly included me into his little clique, his best friends, twins, Alex and Greg Kice. But when it was just me, I was super popular, and super lonely. My only friend after all of the older kids had graduated was my skateboarder buddy, Erin Doom.

Now here I was, back from one year at Seminary, a foreigner, speaking to the "kids" who had been the Juniors and Seniors when I was a Freshman and Sophomore. These were actual adults. I was terrified.

What was even more frightening is that Rich Mullins was there. Of course Rich would be there. He had been a Youth Sponsor in our little Youth Group. Some barefoot, long-haired shoeless hippie guy who played the piano. He had come to Wichita from Indiana to attend Friends College and get his MFA. Little did we know that he would skyrocket to stardom when "Awesome God" from his album: "Winds of Heaven, Stuff of Earth" hit big in 1988. He was just "that singer guy" to us kids back then. And he was there, leaning forward in his chair, long black hair in his deep brown eyes, listening intently.

I don't know what I talked about. It was probably some lesson about Abraham having faith or something "Very Tulsa." You really couldn't live in Tulsa long without hearing something about "FAITH" all the time. Really, there's a "Megachurch" in Tulsa had a huge shield on the top of their church that says "FAITH" – it's a little intimidating. And so there I was, literally an idiot, talking to these fine Kansas folk about my alien Oklahoma teachings, skirting on the edges of heresy. "FAITH" indeed. Did you mean: "Passionately Boring" instead?

Homiletics is the art of preaching... Or the methodology of delivering a sermon, usually in the vein of the Protestant Christian faith. That's what I had signed on for on this night. But no sooner had I begun preaching, did they all begin to ask questions. To my chagrin, I realized that this wasn't a pulpit... It was a lectern. I was not the preacher, I was the Socratic presenter. Where they should have been shouting: "Amen" they were raising their hands and saying: "Well, actually..." I failed at every step. I didn't know how to answer their questions. It was an apologetics nightmare. Those who were trained in asking questions got really nothing back in return for their investment. I failed so hard, one might think I would never grace the stage again.

I don't recall the drive home, I don't recall that week to be frank, but I do recall the next week, when I went to the office supply store, went to their service desk, and picked up some floppies. When I say: "picked up" what I really mean is that I got six or seven of the free AOL starter floppy 3.5 inch diskettes, smiled and waved at the cashier, and left. Alright, I'll be honest, it was theft.

I arrived home, got the scotch tape, covered the read/write window, and reformatted them all. I then proceeded to type poetry. Lots and lots of poetry. A thousand poems.

I must have typed for three or four days straight, for, when I was done, there lay before me six hundred thousand bytes of raw text. Since that filled up most of the capacity of the floppies I had "acquired" – I filled them up, copied them off, decorated them, and gave them to my friends, relatives, and even printed one copy up on paper, at around 350 pages.
If I was not to be a preacher, then I would become a writer. Poetry would be my medium. I could write any subject I wanted to and never worry about peeing my pants on stage ever again.

However, this also won me no awards. Firstly, everyone could tell where the bright yellow diskette had come from... Even after I had peeled away the AOL sticker, and wrote "Paul Hart Poetry" on it.... It was super obvious. Secondly, I had some poignant observations given me about the reality of the writing craft. The poetry was raw and packed with all those "crazy emotions" that good Christians aren't supposed to have. Thirdly, the text itself was a mess. Even if you're a poet, you should be organized.
But coming off of my failure at my preaching gig in Wichita, it felt good to have poured myself into something tangible, where I could measure the results in terms of bytes copied. It was cathartic at the least. I was no wordsmith like Rich Mullins. At least I was honing some sort of ministry craft.

www.ingramcontent.com/pod-product-compliance
Lightning Source LLC
Chambersburg PA
CBHW030153200626
46812CB00016B/1818